MW00772622

THE
SAGAN
DIARY

JOHN SCALZI

SUBTERRANEAN PRESS ✦ 2007

Third Printing

Trade Edition
978-1-59606-103-3

Subterranean Press
PO Box 190106
Burton, MI 48519

www.subterraneanpress.com
www.scalzi.com

For Kristine

COLONIAL DEFENSE FORCES
Internal Security Command
CDF Information Retrieval and Interpretation, 1st Platoon
Col. Michael Blauser, Cmdr

DATE:
241.12.12 SUSN
(see linked table for local equivalents)

FILE NUMBER:
ISC/IRI-003-4530/6(C)

FILE TITLE:
BrainPal Diary, CSF Lt. Jane Sagan (VI)
Phoenix Station, 241.12.07

FILE DESCRIPTION:
See attached note

AUTHOR:
CSF Lt. Jane Sagan (VI)

CLASSIFICATION:
Classified. Security Clearance Level 2 required.

REDACTION:
Lake-Williams algorithm for emotional feed processing.
Emotional feed available as separate file ISC/IRI-003-4530/6(c)(a)

RECORDED BY:
CSF Lt. Jane Sagan (VI)

FILED BY
Lt. Gretchen Schafer, Chief Analyst (SubSpec: Psych), CDF/IRI
CC: Col. Michael Blauser

Preface Note to ISC/IRI-003-4530/6(c), "The Sagan Diary"

Col. Blauser:

As per your instruction in your memorandum of 341.10.07, we have begun processing the BrainPal memory stacks of Colonial Special Forces members who have left that service, whether by death or (rather more rarely) by discharge from service. In both cases BrainPal retrieval was initially via method previously established in our CDF BrainPal retrieval protocol, but per the new directive of 341.10.09 we abandoned physical retrieval of CSF BrainPals and instead began processing BrainPal memory transcriptions as provided by the Special Forces' own IRI office.

Let me reiterate again here in this memorandum what I have expressed to you verbally, which is that processing CSF-provided transcriptions is a massively unsatisfactory solution. The first seven CSF memory stacks we processed were rich in information that we then placed into our analysis matrix, and which were beginning to yield intriguing results before we were ordered to remove the data from the matrix and delete all analyses featuring the data.

Data from the CSF-provided transcriptions have been notably inferior, and while our own forensic scans can show no overt signs that the CSF is tampering with the data, it is my professional opinion that the transcription data have been redacted in some way. I have requested funds and clearance for a more thorough forensic scanning. That request has been in your queue for several days now; I would greatly appreciate a response to it in one way or another.

To give you a sample of the sort of "data" that we are limited to processing at the moment, I am submitting this file, which we have informally been calling "The Sagan Diary." It is a transcription of a series of personal files from the BrainPal of former CSF Lieutenant Jane Sagan, who was discharged from service last week and (somewhat unusually) chose to settle on the established colony world of Huckleberry rather than on Monroe, the colony world set aside for retired Special Forces.

These diary pieces are taken from the last several days before Sagan transferred her consciousness from her Special Forces body to a standard human-template body. I don't need to tell you that for IRI purposes, late-term BrainPal files are typically a gold mine of data, as service members reminisce on their time in service, in doing so refreshing critical data for analysis. Lt. Sagan in particular should be a potentially rich trove of data, as she was present at or participated in several key battles/engagements in the last few years, notably the 2nd Battle of Coral and the Anarkiq offensive; she being Special Forces, she undoubtedly participated in actions which are classified but which, (I would remind those in the Special Forces) we here at IRI are rated to know and view.

Instead, what we have to work with are data-poor bits in which Lt. Sagan thinks about what appears to be a romantic partner of some sort (Cursory investigation suggests a CDF Major, John Perry, who also mustered out of service on the same day and who was on the same shuttle to Huckleberry as Lt. Sagan, accompanied by an unrelated minor, Zoë Boutin. A number of data files for Perry and Boutin are marked classified, which is why I note the investigation was "cursory.").

The diary files are of some anthropological interest, to be sure. It's nice to know Lt. Sagan is in love; Major Perry seems like a lucky fellow. However, for *our* purposes these files are near useless. The only data of analytical note are Sagan's notation of The Third Battle of Provence and the Special Forces retrieval of the *Baton Rouge's* ill-fated Company D, about which of course we have a wealth of information, thanks to all the BrainPals that encounter sent our way, and a discussion of her relationship with prisoner of war named Cainen Suen Su, whose stay with and work for the CDF is classified but otherwise well-documented. Beyond this, the data are thin on the ground.

If I may be frank, Colonel, if the Special Forces are not going to allow us unimpeded access to the BrainPals of its fallen and retired soldiers, then I must question the utility of our processing the data from those BrainPals at all. We process thousands of Brain-Pals in a month, from regular CDF, and we barely have the staff to keep up with that; spinning our wheels processing bogus data from the Special Forces takes up time and processing power we don't have from data which can be of actual use to us. Either we're all working together here or we're not.

Colonel, please read these "diaries" carefully; I'm sure you will come to the same conclusion we have down here in the processing labs. These diaries may be a window into Lt. Sagan's soul, but what we really need is a window into Lt. Sagan's history. I hope the rest of her life turns out the way she wants. Here in the labs, we need more data.

Sincerely,

Lt. Gretchen Schafer, Chief Analyst
(SubSpec: Psych), CDF/IRI

1 WORDS

Words fail me.

There is a disconnect between my mind and my words, between what I think and what I say; not a disconnect in intent but in execution, between the flower of thought and the fruit of the mouth, between the initiation and the completion. I say what I mean but I do not say all that I mean.

I am not speaking to you now. These words do not pass my lips or pass out of my mind. I say them only to myself, forming them perfect and whole and interior, and leaving them on the shelf and closing the door behind me. Others may find these words in time but for now they face only toward me, whispering back my image with full description, golems who write the words of life on my forehead.

These words are my life. Representation of time and counterfeit of emotion, record of loss and celebration of gain. They are not my whole life; words fail me here as they fail anyone, entire worlds slipping through the spaces between words and letters as a life among stars is compressed into this small space. A short life to be sure; and yet long enough to be lost in translation.

But it is enough. Give us a few lines arranged just so and we see a face and more than a face. We see the life behind it; the terrors and ambivalence, the desire and aspiration—intention in a pattern, a person in a coincident assemblage of curves. This is that: A few lines to follow that in themselves mean little but build on themselves; a crystal lattice using absence to suggest presence, the implication of more pregnant in the gaps.

I wish I could show these words to you, you who know me only from outward expression. I wish I could fold these words, package them and present them with a flourish, a rare gift I made of myself to you. But these words do not bend—or rather they will not—or perhaps it is that I cannot find the strength to push them through the doors of my mouth and my mind. They are stubborn words and I fear what would happen if I let them go. They stay inside where you cannot come; they are meant for you, but not sent to you. Words fail me and I return the failure.

But these words exist. These words record, these words stand witness; these words speak, if only to an audience of one. These words are real and they are me, or who I believe I have been; incomplete but truthful, through a mirror darkly but reflecting all the same. I have no doubt that one day you will find these words and that you will find me inside them: a seed to plant in your mind, to become a vine to filigree your memory of who I was and who I was to you. Words fail me but I will use them anyway. And in their failure and despite their failure I will live again and you will love me again, as you love me now.

◆◆◆

You do not remember your birth but I remember mine. I remember the sudden shock of consciousness, awareness flinging itself at me and demanding to be embraced, and me not knowing enough to do anything other than embrace it back. I sometimes wonder if I had a choice, or if I could have known then what I know now, if I would have received its embrace or would have punched it in the throat, and sent it staggering away to pester someone else, to leave me alone in a newborn senescence from which I would not awake. But in this we are all alike, those who remember our birth and those who do not: None of us asked to be born.

I awoke in perfect awareness and to a voice in my head which spoke "You are Jane Sagan," and with those words the electric pricking of context, describing the relationship of "you," and of "are" and of "Jane" and of "Sagan"—putting together the words like pieces of spontaneously generated puzzle, and then clicking them into place so the puzzle made sense, even if we later discovered how much we really hated puzzles.

But the words were a lie. I wasn't Jane Sagan at all; I was a changeling, a creature stolen to take the place of someone else. Someone I did not know nor would ever know, someone whose entire life had been set aside for the mere utility of her genes, everything she ever was reduced to a long chemical strand—adenine, thymine, cytosine and guanine—the abrupt tattoo of these four notes replacing a symphony of experience. She was dead but she would not be allowed to rest, because I was needed here.

I wonder if she was in this body before me, if before my consciousness was dropped in this head she waited sleeping, dreaming of her life before and dreaming of her life to come. I wonder if she's dreaming still, housed in the interstices and the places in my mind I do not go. If she is here I wonder if she resents me for taking her place, or whether she is glad of the company, and enjoys the world through my eyes. I cannot tell.

But I dream of her. I dream she and I stand at her grave, standing apart with the headstone between us, close enough to touch although we never do. And she says "Talk to me" and I do, trying to explain a warrior's life to a woman who never fought, ashamed that I have nothing to share with her but death, which she already knows more about than I.

But she smiles and I know that she doesn't begrudge me that. I ask her to tell me about her and she does and speaks of home and children and of a life of connection, things I have not possessed in my own life but which she is happy to share. I wake up and her words dissipate, specifics evaporating and leaving behind a memory of comfort.

I dreamt of her before we met but I will not tell you that.

◆ ◆ ◆

The name "Jane Sagan." The name itself mere words: The first name bland and common, the second name for a scientist who hoped for a better universe than the one we live in. I wonder if he were alive what he would think of the woman who used it now, and the cosmos in which she finds herself; whether he could embrace one or both, see beauty in either, or only entropy and slight regard; a rebuke on his lips for this demon-haunted world.

If he demanded his name back it would not matter. The name was random first and last, provided from a list designed to make sure only one Special Forces soldier owned a name at a time. There would not be another Jane Sagan until I bled my life away in battle, the name floating up off my corpse like the spirit of a Buddhist, to be reincarnated on the Wheel of Suffering: returning but learning nothing, repeating the same lessons again and once more, its owners torn from life on different worlds but performing the same actions.

My name is random but I earned it in time. I became Jane Sagan not through the whim of convention but through breathing and moving and fighting and discovering love—each of these coring through the undifferentiated mass of my existence, paring away that which was not me, shedding what was not essential and sometimes what was, demanding I retrieve what I lost or accept its loss; the diminution of a self only recently defined and still defining itself.

I lost some of what I should have been and could have been for you. The parts of me that I lent others who then left me unwillingly or willingly, as they earned the names they had, even as those names lifted up from them, their purpose spent—those which they signified already fading against the violence of bone and metal.

They took part of me with them. I kept part of them with me, to become me in the fullness of time, some of who I could have been replaced by all that was left of them. If you looked you could have seen them in me: discrete objects breaking down, atoms that would not willingly cohere to the molecule, a colloidal suspension of memory and more than memory; part of me and held within me, bound by names they no longer claimed but becoming me, to be called by my name, "Jane Sagan."

In the end I am who I am. I am what I have made myself and what has been made of me. Part of who I am is who you are too; I have given you me as well. I would take your name and hold it in me, and whisper my name in your ear.

2 KILLING

I am not Death. I am killing; I am the verb, I am the action, I am the performance. I am the movement that cuts the spine; I am the mass which pulps the brain. I am the headsnap ejecting consciousness into the air.

I am not Death but she follows close behind, the noun, the pronouncement, the dénouement and the end. She looks for where I have gone next, and where she is needed, and sometimes where she is wanted; desired as the worlds for those whom I have visited narrow down to a point too heavy to be long borne.

I have wondered whether death collapses the point into nothingness or expands it into eternity, but I do not wonder long. Death follows me but I do not look back to her and I do not dwell on what she does. I am killing, I am the action, and I have a job to do.

I am connected to those I kill: a T-shaped joint where their lives intersect mine, the line of their lives terminating in the contact while mine continues on to the next orthogonal encounter, toward the promise and threat of becoming the terminating arm—of the moment when death no longer follows but stands pitilessly before me, expanding or contracting everything I ever was or will be for her own unknowable aims.

I am connected to those I kill and I long to know them. I long to look down their line to see what has led them to me; whether they chose this moment or had it chosen. If they had chosen it, whether it was love or honor or duty or something else that set their line toward mine; if they had it chosen why they chose to accept it, and whether they would have accepted the choice if they knew I was waiting for them, preparing their final moment, every possible future imploding toward the point of my knife, the grain of my bullet, the grip of my hand.

I am connected to those I kill and would look past them, down the line of their lives to the originating point, to the other T-joint where their lives intersect with another: to the creature who bore them—to the woman, the female, the she; the verb and action and performance to complement my own, she who is not birth but whose acts allowed it, as I am not death but whose acts permit it.

When she first held this child who would become what I would kill, did she look for me as I look for her? Did she see me across the line of a life yet un-lived? I want to know how I would appear to her: the anti-mother to kill whom she had created, or perhaps a crossbeam with her, to support the entirety of a life, without whom that life would be useless.

I do not flatter myself to suggest she would approve of what I represent, of what I would do, will do, have done, to the life she created and cherished. But I wonder if she would understand I am connected to her, through the one she bore. I stand facing her, staring across the chasm of time forded by this life between us.

◆◆◆

The first thing I killed was unspeakable. Its species had a name for itself spoken like a hammer thumping onto meat; we could not have spoken it if we had tried.

We did not try. We called them for their language, for the percussive explosions which passed for their speech and filled the air when we fought them, like the beating of heavy skins. They were talking drums with weapons.

They were Thumpers and they were our enemy,

our nemesis for the crime of landing on a world we said we owned and begging to differ with us on the matter. We sent emissaries to negotiate with them: 16th Brigade, Company D on the ship *Baton Rouge*. The negotiations did not go well. The *Baton Rouge* was made to fall into the atmosphere in a sparkling show, as metal and men tore into the sky and the sky tore back, shearing them down in layers that grew into conical sections of ash expanding behind their shrinking mass, ignored by the members of Company D on the skin of the world, who could not look up from their battle to see their friends' farewell.

We felt Company D deserved its fate, the negotiations a lie and stupidly done at that; ham-handed arrogance that had gotten them stuck, and pleading for our help. We called them the "The Idiots"; we would have left them to die—an object lesson in incompetence—but we were not allowed a vote. We found ourselves on a world we should not have been on, to retrieve those who should not have needed retrieval, to kill those whose lives we should have not been made to take.

We would not complain about it. This was what we were bred to do. But it did not change the fact; my first mission was fighting someone else's battle, making it my own by necessity. There was not much of Company D to retrieve; just enough for someone above us to declare victory despite the dead we left behind.

I will not detail the battle. I am here and that is enough.

The first thing I killed danced when I killed it, the force of the bullet spreading across its surface even as the slug traveled through its mass. It danced and spun and twisted and fell, shedding blood in a spiraling helix, angular momentum and gravity bartering for its movement and gravity getting the better end of the deal. It fell and lay sodden and I moved on to the next, already the verb and the action, already movement and purpose. My body moved.

My mind stayed, and in quiet moments in the days that followed returned to the dance, to the spin and slide and the sound of mortality the thing thumped out as it fell. I returned to that sound and imagined what it said: a shout of pain, a brief tattoo of regrets, the name of a lover or a brother or perhaps a mother; a final call backward, a farewell to the one who had given it life or those who filled the life with joy, not to be seen again in the time that remained.

I have the moment recorded. If I chose I could open that moment again, find a translation and know for certain. I choose not to know. I had killed this

thing. It deserved to have its final words fly past me, to find those for whom they were meant.

◆◆◆

I think on what I owe those I kill. Clearly I do not owe them their lives, nor do I owe them individual memory; I have killed far too many to mark each with remembrance. My time with nearly all is too short to note much other than that they are dead and I am alive, even if it was a near thing on both counts.

I do not owe them guilt or regret. I have done what I have done. I know what I have done well and what I have done poorly, and for whatever I might be judged, I know no one knows better than I for what things I should be called into account. I know my own measure and will not burden those whom I have killed. If they have souls let them go to where they are bound, without my pleas of forgiveness to chain them to me, and to this world.

What I owe those I kill is understanding. I owe them the courtesy of recognition; acknowledgement that they were something other than just another thing I had to kill on the way to other things I had to kill. I cannot know every creature I have killed; I cannot spare the memory for each of them entire. But I will not pretend they were not my equal. Their lives were their own, and in their way they loved and feared and wondered and hoped. They did not expect me to be the end of all of that.

I will not pretend that all there was to them was the flesh I wounded, the bones I shattered, the blood I made to spill. I will not pretend that it does not matter to them that their lives are at an end. I grieve the loss of those I love and I will not pretend that those I kill are not missed, were not loved, are not grieved.

Some would not choose to do this and I do not fault them. Each of us does what we can to accept ourselves and what we do. But to see those I kill as less than myself lessens myself. I do not have enough of myself to lose that way.

After my first mission I learned of the Thumpers: their culture and ways and world. I learned of their gods and demons, their myths and fables and stories, learned of their art and song and the dances they danced without a bullet to guide them. I became an expert on the creatures I had killed, and when I did the one I made to dance and die took its leave of me.

I learned of the next people I would kill before I killed them, as I have done every time since. It became my job, along with killing, to learn what I could about those we fought and killed, the better to fight them, and the better to kill them—my need to know and understand and recognize those whose lives I end turned to practical use.

It is good to be useful for more than just killing. It is better to know that in my way I honor those I kill, as I would hope they would honor me.

3 SPEAKING

Let me speak your name. Let me feel the movement of my tongue within my mouth, of lips stretched and jaw pushed slightly forward, of the breath from my lungs shaped and formed into noise and phonemes and syllables and words; into proper nouns signifying you. Two names with marvelous utility: to recall you from memory, to bid for your attention, to speak your identity into the air and in doing so affirm you in your tangible skin, with vibration and waves and exhalation, with the intimacy of sound spoken aloud; with the pleasure that comes from the physical act of declaring you.

Let me speak your name and in speaking let me sing, a secret melody whose notes rise like birds and fall into your ears, to turn you toward me, with a smile that anticipates your own hidden song that choruses with my name. Let me speak your name so I may hear my name spoken to me from you.

You cannot imagine the sensuousness of speech, you who have spoken all your life, you who have mouthed words like bread, a staff of life common on your tongue. You cannot appreciate the luxury speech represents to those of us who have no time for it, we who speed our words, transmitting mind to mind without mediation, not even the briefest pause between mind and mouth to temper what we say or to soften sharp edges.

To speak without words is to speak fast and cheap, to not have to choose words either wisely or poorly but to send them all without discrimination—all content and no style, function over form, everything being what is said and nothing being how it is said. I talk to those I know, one mind to another, efficient and sure. We say what we need to say and then move on. Words do not mean to us what they mean to you and yours. We have other ways to share our emotions and our care and regard. Words do not carry that freight for us; they are light and fast and hollow. Sparrows with fragile bones.

Your words are not like this. Your words are filled, their hollows crammed with meaning, things unsaid nested within, jammed with implication. It is a wonder they do not drop to the floor the moment they leave your mouth. I marvel at what you say and even more how you say it, how your words shift their shape and contain their intent until they are inside me and unpack their contents, to leave me in awe of their economy. So much said with so little.

I cannot do this myself. We speak the same language but build our words differently. Mine are simple and deliberate, yours effortlessly complex. You are not aware of the miracles you make of your words. I cannot do this myself; I do not even try, save when I am speaking your name. With those few words I am your equal, filling the words with complexity and light. Stained glass shining from the inside.

You are so used to what you do with your words that you do not notice the effort I put into mine. I don't mind. Take for granted that your name flows from my lips. It is a gift to me that you expect it there. Let me speak your name and fulfill your expectation.

I was not always in love with the spoken word. Those of you born to speech do not know how you tax the patience of those of us born to thought—how our first thought in hearing one of you speak is to wonder at the extent of your damage, to be curious at what sort of trauma could result in such an obvious and slow moving thing such as stands before us. We listen with politeness and internal pity: You cannot be faulted for the deficiencies to which you are born, and we would not choose to point out that they exist.

We listen and wait for our turn to speak, and then speak as slowly as you have been afflicted to do so. We try to get done with it as quickly as possible, because we know how much your sort wish to speak again, straining to pass along information along with asides and anecdotes and digressions and irrelevancies, leaving us to filter what you mean from what you say (We are no less verbose but at least we are quicker, when we talk among ourselves through our thoughts). And when you are done, again we speak, briefly and with economy and to the point, speaking what need be said and ignoring that which does not. For our courtesy we are labeled arrogant and curt. It annoys us.

In time I came to appreciate the spoken word, with its implications and intimations and allusions, with its potential of saying more than mere words, its palette of meaning richer and wider than I first grasped. And with that appreciation came exasperation at those gifted with speaking, who could say so much with what they said and how they said it, and chose to say nothing of consequence; who opened their mouth and allowed banality to fall out and thud to the ground; who were unaware that they could do with their words with the barest minimum of effort what I with all my desire could accomplish only haltingly, if at all. It was like being starved and watching those at a feast ignore the best dishes to fill up on bread.

If I could have I would have pushed their faces into their words, to make them see the parody they made of them. But they would have only have been confused and I would only have been more exasperated. There is a saying along the lines of not trying to teach a pig to sing because it wastes your time and annoys the pig. I want you to know how many times I have stood in pig-filled rooms, and longed to annoy.

I did not. I sat and listened to them talk instead, and was amazed to discover more in their words: subtext and overtones, emotional resonances that even those speaking did not know were there, the rhythm and pattern and tone of their speech opening them wide to be read. Books whose messages are not in the text but the footnotes. A library of the human experience.

It took time to translate the language, and I do not imagine I have mastered it. It will never be my native tongue. But I hear it well enough that in hearing it I see those who speak it anew, and once again I have pity for those who speak aloud. Not because they speak so slowly but because so many of them are deaf to all that they say. If they could hear what I hear they would be amazed.

◆◆◆

My native tongue is not a tongue but the flash of neurons decoded and transmitted by machine instead of muscle. But it is my tongue nonetheless: my tongue, my map, my window, my apprehension of the world to myself. I am leaving it behind to be with you. I am an immigrant whose first language will not be simply unused but amputated, the parts of me I used to speak it left behind, no part of who I will be to speak it, even in the silence of my mind.

You do not know how this worries me. It is not that I am to be made to speak aloud a language I love and long to hear but which I speak imperfectly. In time I will speak it well enough. I worry that who I am is in how I know to speak; that I am shaped by my words and how I say them, and that in my deprivation, that which is me will diminish and become something other than what I am and what I am to you.

I am doing something new. I am holding myself in my mind—who I have been and who I am—wordless and silent; no description to resolve into a lexicon spoken or sent, a view of myself immune to travel or translation or amputation. When I move to your world my thoughts will be filled with myself; the measure of my character and deficiencies and desires held mute and in being mute held whole, so that when I am sent to you, I will be who I have been and who I am, so I can be who I will become with you.

I know you would not begrudge me this, that you would want me to think on myself if by doing so I believed that it would keep me myself. But you should know that as I hold myself in my thoughts, to will myself into being myself once more, the version of me I hold to myself holds you in her thoughts. She holds you wordlessly: who you have been and who you are, and who you will become with her. She holds you in her without words or speech and longs to speak your name.

4 FRIENDSHIP

I rose early the day I killed my friend. I knew that when I killed him I would have to be ready, could not hesitate or be moved by his suffering, but be ready to strike swift and sure, and for that I needed to prepare myself. I needed not to harden myself but to be strong enough to hold myself open, to measure his pain not with detachment but with empathy, to strike him at the precise moment when the balance between his will and his suffering tumbled irretrievably against him; to allow him his struggle but not to struggle needlessly. I was to honor his final moments by judging when they would be, to do what he would not be able to do, and to give him the honor he was due from me and for himself. I rose early and spent the day in silence, and when I was ready and when the time had come, I took my knife and I went to him.

He did not answer his door; it was too late for that. His disease was untreated and untrammeled, sending the impulses of his nerves to bleed into his flesh, to twitch the muscle and fritter away any semblance of control. A friend let me enter and drew me to the rough mat on the floor, on which our friend sat and shook. I knelt in front of my friend and greeted him; drew my knife for him to see and placed it between us, not as a threat but as a promise, fulfillment of his request and my requirement to end his life.

He turned his head toward the knife and reached out a palsied hand to touch it, jostling it slightly as he did so. Told me it would serve, then reached the same hand to me, bidding me to take it. I found that I could not, the hand holding itself up for long seconds before retreating to its owner.

You blame yourself for this still, said my friend. You blame yourself for this disease you gave me, the one that will kill me today. It sits between us like an unwelcome guest.

I will not ask you to absolve yourself of this guilt. You have willingly picked it up and placed it on your shoulders. Only you will be able to set it down again. But know that I do not ask you to carry it for me. I would not have you think you are unworthy to touch my hand, you who are the only one I can trust and who I will trust in this final hour.

You afflicted me with this disease, took me far from my home and far from the people I love, and

brought me to this moment. But you have also called me friend, understood me, and have given me honor and do me great honor now.

You have been long forgiven by me, and all that I would have between us now is companionship and love. You are my last and best friend. Remember that when your burden of guilt weighs you down.

◆◆◆

And with those words my friend fell silent, curled himself small and began his wait, holding himself to himself as his body betrayed itself, scattering the messages between body and mind, pushing arms and legs, contorting his silent contemplation into a jester's pantomime, making a mockery of his dignity—but not so much a mockery that his dignity did not hold.

It was hard to watch him leak and spasm and grunt. But I would not turn away. I watched every moment, silent and observant, owing him witness for the affliction I gave him and the release I would yet give him, until the moment when I became aware with every sense that my friend had arrived at his moment of release. I did not hesitate. I picked up my knife and prepared to find his heart.

There is a moment of surface tension when a knife blade presents its demand and the flesh honors it. An instant of pressure before the puncture, the rip before the slide, a small eternity easy to miss but impossible to ignore if you've felt it before. I lived in that moment a great while for the small sliver of time it was there.

And then I moved on, angled my blade in and up, felt its tip pierce its target and slide through the other side, and continued on until the flat of the hilt rested cold on his chest. I moved in close and embraced him, the better to provide leverage to twist the blade, and make the argument to his heart that its work was forever done. The heart did not argue and for that I was grateful.

My friend gripped me as I gripped him, exhaling at the crystal clarity of the knife, cutting through his diffuse and random pain to rally every thought in his body, every final message that coursed along his nerves, toward the goal of reaching his hand to me a second and final time.

I took it and held it, and wet it with my tears as I bent to kiss it, an action which surprised me and released me, and let me lay my burden down. I'm sure my friend saw it in his failing last moment of life; his last gift to me and my last gift to him, so that all that was between us in the end was companionship and love. He died in my arms and holding my hand, and after a minute I set him down on his rough mat, stepped back to where his other friend stood waiting, and gave our friend's soul space to depart.

◆◆◆

I did not say goodbye to my friend then, but some time later, as I held his body in my hands, floating in the cold and dark above the brilliant green world of his birth. A place I had come to fulfill a promise: to see him home, to return him to a place from which my actions had kept him while he was still alive. It was not easy to get there and it would not be easy to return, but I had risked my own death for reasons far more trivial. I would not shame my friend or myself by denying him his return home, because it would be inconvenient for me to take him there.

And so I floated above this great green world, body in hand, holding it longer than I should have, whispering words to it that would not carry in the vacuum but which I said nonetheless, before letting it go and releasing it to spiral into the gravity well of my friend's childhood world. My friend and I paced each other a while, sharing the same orbit, until I turned to make my way back to my own world. I did not turn back to see my friend fall away from me. I had said my goodbyes and was content to let him find his own way home.

I wonder if as he fell those he had loved felt him return home and felt his absence filled, as he shot across the sky and spread himself in it. I like to think they did, not because I am the one who took him from them, but because I loved him too, and in loving him felt his love for them. I hope they looked to the sky, saw him move through it, and were glad to have him home.

5 AGE

When you were born all you could do was cry. When I was born I woke to a whisper, giving me a name and telling me to come away from my cradle. I walked, one foot and then another, understanding fully without understanding how I understood. I turned to see my birthmates, all walking and all sending out their own names, and receiving names in turn. We were born and we were aware and we would soon be made to fight.

Our childhoods did not exist, except perhaps in the moment between being given our names and setting our feet on the ground. Once that step was taken we had a purpose, a call to action. We answered it unthinkingly, unaware of our options or that there were options—that concept left packed up for the time being because that was what was required in the moment—no more mind than it took to walk, one foot and then another, into the rest of our lives.

When you were two you had learned to speak and walk. When I was two I was made an officer—a lieutenant—to replace the one whose body had been bisected in front of me, dorsal and ventral peeling away from each other and falling sideways, the last thought he sent one of surprise at feeling a cool breeze between his front and back. And I, stumbling back with wounds of my own, holding my arm across my abdomen to keep my insides in, at an age when you were pulling the heads off your sister's dolls.

When you were four you learned to read and tie your shoes. When I was four I attempted to negotiate a surrender, to keep my soldiers from having to risk their lives by having to take a settlement one hut at a time. There was no surrender and we went through the settlement, killing as we went and dying too, needless deaths all around, needless save to honor the death wish of the settlement leader, who preferred annihilation to life. I made sure I found him, denied him the martyrdom he imagined for himself, made him bury his dead, and gave him a cell to live a life which I hoped would be long enough to sprout regret.

When you were six you sat in school and learned to add two and three. When I was six I found you, or what remained of you—so much of you strewed behind you, along with the wreckage of your ship and your crew, and what was left of you alive only through luck and will and technology. You should have been dead when we met, and you should have died after we met, in the long minutes between finding you and saving you.

I remember touching your face and lying to you that you were all right now, seeing you weep and wondering if it might not be more merciful to let you die. But I had my orders to bring you back, so I did, knowing what it would mean for your life but not knowing what it would mean for mine. I was six when I met the person I would love, and became the person you would love again: the person I was made from, whom you met, or so you told me, when you were six.

◆◆◆

Please understand me. I do not mean to belittle you when I note that I was leading soldiers at an age when you could barely control your bladder, or that I stood dazzled by three moons rising over a phosphorescent sea, lacking the poetry to match in my head the song in my eyes, at an age where you enjoyed the taste of paste and boogers and small coins.

You no more chose how to be born than I did, and your life is no more or less complete because you required two decades to become an adult, and several decades after that to become a soldier, both of which I was from the moment I opened my eyes. I do not mean to demean you when I admit I find some amusement at the idea of you as a child, of you reaching no higher than my waist, of you big-eyed, and your big head wobbly on your neck, looking at the world with curiosity if not comprehension, needing to wait years to know enough to know how little you know.

I note these differences because they stand between us. When you speak of growing up and growing old, you speak to someone who did not do the first, and can choose not to fear the second. Every day of my life from first to this, in a body that defies both growth and decay, even if one day it cannot defy death. It is not eternal but it doesn't change, and if I chose I could stay in it for as long as I could manage. Timeless in my way, unyielding to both creation and destruction, and because of this separate from the human stream of age—the arc that bends from development to deconstruction, that gives definition to your days, provides sense of story and an assurance of all things in their season, and all of it coming to an end as natural and complete as its beginning.

I hear you speak of your childhood as the blind hear someone speak of the color of a flower or of a beloved's eyes; understanding that the color exists, understanding the emotion color can arouse, but lacking the experience that brings understanding into empathy, understanding a thing without feeling it deep in the brain, where the joy of it will shudder out, down the nerves to one's very fingertips.

Childhood is a country undiscoverable to me, something so far removed from me that I cannot even say that it was denied, because it was never something that I was meant to have. Nor is it something I desire, whose absence I resent. I am who I am and that is enough. It is simply that childhood is an experience we do not share, another place where our lives refuse to link, a commonality we do not have. When I think of you as a child it amuses me, and it makes me sad that you do not get to think of me the same way.

◆◆◆

I am nine years old. In those nine years I have seen things that others could spend lifetimes and never once see. I have traveled farther than entire millennia of explorers, their journeys laid end to end and back again. I have been on more worlds than we knew could possibly exist for all but the smallest slice of time our species stared up at the stars. I have measured a life not in teaspoons or tablespoons or ladles or jugs but in inexhaustible gouts of experience, pushing me forward into wonder and terror and being.

I am nine years old and I have lived in every moment of that life. No time wasted in idleness and futility, in routine and repetition, in grinding gears or marking time. You can't tell me I have lived less than those who have merely lived longer.

It does not matter: All these experiences and all this experience make no difference in how I am seen—how all of us are seen, those of us whose lives who begin *in medias res*. I am nine years old and must be what they remember nine-year-olds to be, seen, at best, as an idiot savant, a useful moron, a little girl in a big girl's body.

Those who don't belittle me fear me, me and mine; grown too fast, made too smart, too far out of their own experience to understand, assumed to be without morals because they would not have been moral at the same age. We are sent to do the things they judge necessary and yet fear to do—fine for us to be given tasks that might cost us our souls when we're assumed not to have souls at all. We learn quickly not to hold this fear and stupidity against most of the human race, because the alternative is to let you all die.

When I first decided to love you I needed to know how you would see me. Whether you like so many others would see a child in an oversized body, or someone who was your equal in everything but time. I waited for the moment of condescension, for the casual dismissal, for the instance when you would ask what I could possibly know, given how little time I could have known it in.

I am waiting still, but I no longer expect its arrival. You are not blind to my age or our differences; you know better than anyone how brief my existence has been, because my life could have only begun after her life ended. Perhaps you see me as a continuation of a life interrupted, or perhaps you simply don't care and see me as your equal because there is no reason not to. I have time to find out as our lives continue, and we mark time not by what has come before, but by what we have together.

6 SEX

I must apologize to you. I am sitting with you and you are talking to me, telling me about the world to which we are going, where you and I will start our lives together. I'm sure what you're saying is important—critical things I need to know, about a place I have never been but where I will spend the rest of my days. I am sure you are telling me things I need to hear, but I must confess I'm not hearing a single word.

Instead I am intent on your face, and the movement of your lips, and the memory of how those lips feel when they are on me. While you speak I am thinking of the last time we kissed, and the subtle friction that took place because we were so slightly out of sync, the rush of blood flooding our lips to make them softer, and make us more aware of just how many nerve endings each of us were pressing against the other.

Your words arrive at ears that are not deaf but disinterested, because although what you say is something I need to know, I know I can make you repeat it some other time. You will oblige me that way. And so I watch your lips purse and thin and tighten and repeat, knowing that the same motions can be used for other ends, and enjoying the memory of those ends achieved.

I apologize now because I am staring at your hands, which you use as punctuation—another layer of language to illustrate the point you think I am hearing, but which in reality is flying past my head and falling into piles against the wall behind me. I realize that this is not like me, that you prize my seriousness and my ability to focus. You should know I am serious and I am focused, just not on what you'd prefer me to be. It is your hands that have my attention now, their short and choppy movements at the moment belying their startling fluidity as they move over me, and their strength when they lock with mine and press them down as you press your body into me.

There is an argument to be made as to which of us is stronger, but in the moment is not the time for that. Your strength is a sign of your intent and your request that I honor that intent. I've made the same request, and in the same way. I remember that you've honored it as well, hands locked and pressed and then released, to move with intent, another layer of language, to illustrate a point I want to hear.

I apologize yet again. This is a total loss. I am so far downstream from whatever it is that you've said that it would be impossible to catch up, and besides I am focused on other topics, about which I intend to make you presently aware. I am sorry that I have been entirely lost in your lips and hands and the memories of each on me. But you should know that I am going to make it up to you, and let you put them to what I feel is better use than the service to which they are put now. I think you will agree that all things considered, the purpose I have for them is a better one for all involved.

Even so I apologize for the inattention. I also apologize for surprising you just now, by knocking aside the table inconveniently set between us. And now I must apologize for upsetting your chair with you still in it, and for knocking your head on the floor. I will do what I can to make you forget your pain.

◆◆◆

Sex with you is unlike any other sex I've had. I do not say this like one of the restless virgins of literature, swept up in swooning tides of bliss. I am not the swooning type. And while you are good, you are not that good; your mere touch is not enough to transport me to fantastical realms of ecstasy, or whatever ridiculous phrase one would use to express such an idea.

Sex is not a holy or sacred thing or a physical machine to express a separate emotion. I fuck to enjoy myself and to celebrate the fact I am alive. I understand the idea of making love, but it seems a bad way to go about it. I don't fuck to show my love. I love to show my love and let the fucking be its own thing. I love you and I love fucking you and I have no need to complicate either with the other. They are both true statements and they are both good. I am content to have them remain that way.

My sex before you was with my own, with those born as I was, who communicate as I do, equally adept at transmitting sensation and emotion whole and unrefined, over the same line as we send words. With us sex is not a matter simply of bodies, and of a pantomime approximation of knowing if what you are doing is working for those you are with. You feel what they feel and they feel what you feel, a positive feedback loop to take every thrust and pull and lick and touch, and magnify it until your nerves ring with your exhaustion, and the exhaustion of your partners.

It is needless to say what fun it can be. But it's also worth noting what it lacks. Being inside someone's head heightens the performance, and it makes you aware it is a performance: moves choreographed to increase pleasure, focused on the mechanics of sex but lacking in connection, ironic when you consider that your lover is inside your head as much as inside your body.

The first time we were together, I sent toward you to bind our thoughts and realized that your mind was shut to me; that not once had your mind been as open as your body. That you had lacked that dimension in your sex and always had. I pitied you. And then you put your mouth on me, and your hands, and I had nothing to do but focus on how you moved on me, and against me, and inside me.

And I realized that you lacked nothing; that in place of feeling your thoughts reflected in mine, I felt your desire and your inescapable need to be inside of me, not only with your body and not with your mind, but with every particle of your soul. I laughed and came at the same time, and wept as I tried to devour you, to own you and be every part of you as much as I was myself.

It was something I had never done before and will not do with anyone else. You opened me to desire, and I desire not to desire anyone but you.

◆◆◆

I regret to say that we have made a mess of the room, but I do not regret to say that you are inside of me. We will reconstruct the room later, but for now I want to focus on what we are doing, which makes me wonder why I am bothering to narrate this in my own head, observing me observing you inside of me.

Now I remember. I'm observing this because I want you to know how I know the nature of desire, that I have learned it from you, and that I question whether desire is truly what I feel. I have taken the time to read on the nature of desire and have learned the physiology of it—the rush of chemicals through the brain, tunneling pathways and new connections. But among this physiology, the psychology, the warning that desire does not stay, that novelty wanes and desire wanders, looking for someone new to attach to, or simply wanders off leaving behind something else that may be as satisfying in its way, but is not desire.

If this is true then I am not now feeling desire. What I feel for you has not wandered or waned or lessened, but has grown since the first time you pressed your mouth to mine and served your notice that you had desires of your own. I look at you now even as you are between me, and would push you farther into me until there is no space between us, no gap between where I stop and you begin, but a continuum and a binding, covalent and irrevocable. If it is not desire I do not know what to call it, save to call it love, which I already feel in different ways than this.

I am without a word to describe what I feel, if it is not desire and is not love. So I will express it how I can, not in words but in action, with lips and hands and bodies and merging, with sex and fucking and release.

I have never been inside someone as deeply as I am inside you. I love to feel you inside me, the physical complement to my spiritual state, expression made flesh of what I would say to you if I had the words. I press you into me, and draw into a kiss the lips that earlier had been speaking. I take the hands that had earlier moved in the air and bid you move them on me. Later you will tell me again what you had earlier said, and I will listen then, I promise.

But for now all I can say is that I apologize for wanting you, and in wanting you having you. And I apologize in advance for all the times I will want you between now and the end of our lives. If you can find it in your heart to forgive me I will make it worth your while, and will forgive you for all the times you will want me, and will accept your apologies, as you accept mine now.

7 FEAR

Fear enters the room and sits down in a chair and with a polite smile asks to open negotiations. Fear is small and hard and patient, and duplicitous, because in asking to negotiate it knows I cannot refuse. I am obliged to accommodate Fear because I am human, and no human is without fear. Fear sits and smiles and is predatory, immobile and silent and serene; an observer who conserves his energy and is content to wait. We watch each other and take our measures, he to undo me and me to avoid being undone. We both sit and measure and stare. And then because I long for other company, I ask him to show me what I should fear.

To begin he offers me the fear of death, and I laugh. I laugh because I know Death far too well to fear her. Death is my intimate and my companion; I am her messenger and handmaiden. We have walked too many worlds and have become too familiar; close acquaintances if not friends, because you can never befriend Death without embracing her, and for now I keep her at a safe and prudent distance. Even so I know her methods and her means and her agenda. I know her legendary capriciousness is overstated but that her inevitability is not. Death comes to us all, even those who have served her so well.

It is foolish to fear the inevitable. I know I will die. Fearing Death will not make her come for me later and might send me to her sooner, when a blind rush from her sends me into her arms. I will not fear her and I will not fear going to her when it is time to do so. I tell Fear to show me something else.

He shows me Pain, myriad as Death is singular, creative in his attention-seeking, and in his desire to overwhelm every scrap of consciousness. The most perfect of egotists.

I am not impressed. Pain is a tool: a diagnostic instrument in one's self, a lever in others, and in all things symbolic of something else that better deserves our attention. Pain may represent Death, who I refuse to fear. Pain may represent power, which I also refuse to fear; I am better than those who would use their power to make me fear them, power predicated on the assumption that I will do anything simply to exist. They presume to hold my life in trust; my regret as I would end my life would be that I would not be there as they realized how little power they had over me. I choose not to fear the things Pain represents, leaving pain a process, a signal, a firing of nerves to be endured.

✦✦✦

Of course Fear knows all this. Knows that I fear neither Death nor Pain, or those who use either to divorce me from my will. This is what fear does: presents you with what you can bear, so that when he shows you what is unbearable, you will open wider to let him feed on your heart. I know this and even knowing this does not keep me from a moment of satisfaction, and the hope that Fear will step away from my table. Fear allows you a moment to hope that he doesn't truly know what will break you. But he does, and he proves it to me by showing me you, and showing you without me.

This is what I fear. And I confess that part of me hates you a little for it, hates that you have taken my life and so threaded it with yours that I can't pull away without losing myself; I who had always been whole in myself but who now knows what she stands to lose in losing you.

It is not your death I fear, or separation. We have been at war as long as we have known of each other.

Death follows behind us both, and separation has been what we have had the most of, our time together both trivial and precious measured against our time in absence. Death and separation do not alter what is between us. What I fear is diminishment, and subtle change, and the moment in which a life without you becomes a sustainable thought.

It seems such a small thing compared to all the other things one may fear. There is no finality here; you and I would continue in our lives, no death or distance to separate us. Just disinterest, and the perception of what we have becoming what we once had, becoming memory and history and remembrance. What was separated from what is and separate from what will be.

A small thing and a survivable thing. And for all that the thought of it falls on me like wreckage and pulls into me to burn with sickening violence. I look across the table and Fear is gone, not because it has gone but because it has found the thing that will let it live in me. I fear a life without you and you without me.

◆◆◆

I choose not to share this fear with you. You do not deserve to have it put on you. There has never been a time when you have not reached toward me, even when I had pushed you away (or, when we were formally introduced, when I threw you across a table). You never made me ask your forgiveness for being her, and you never loved me simply because I was the only part of her you had left. You have always seen me and you have always seen me with you.

I feel ashamed I have this fear, based on nothing real, called into existence by my own irrationality. I have so many excuses for it, beginning with my youth, and my inexperience in weaving my life to someone else's. But I will not rationalize this fear. It is what it is; the serpent in my ear, whispering the promise of the fall.

I am human. Fear lives in me and sets to make my heart bitter. But I know something about Fear. Fear is a scavenger who feeds on the future; on what may be and what is possible, extending down the line of our lives. Fear lives in me and I cannot change that. But I choose to starve Fear. I choose to live here with you now.

In the future perhaps we will diminish and we will divide, and all we will have is memory. I accept that this could be what we have in time, and in accepting it set it aside. What is left to me is this moment, and you with me. I choose to be with you in this moment, to love you in the present time and in the present tense. It is all the time we have, have ever had, or will ever have. All of our lives here and now, wher-ever here and whenever now may be.

I love you now and will not regret having loved you and will not fear loving you forward. I am here now and I am with you. It is enough for as long as I have it.

With that thought I accept what I must from Fear and move toward you. Negotiations are closed, and you and I remain.

8 ENDINGS

It is time to come to the end of things and to the beginning.

I am standing in a room where there are two of me. One of them is who I have always been as long as I have had memory of myself. The other is who I will be, someone I will be poured into to become who I must be to start our lives together.

I cannot stop staring at her. I see myself in the curve of her cheek and the line of her nose and the length of her limbs. Through her I will gain many things I would not have.

I will gain a husband and a daughter and a new world, which I will not have to meet at the end of a gun, and whose citizens I will not have to defend or kill. I will gain a measure of peace and I will gain an identity that is my own—not one of a soldier or an officer or a killer, but simply Jane Sagan, whoever she may be.

She offers me so many things, she who is not yet me. And all I have to do for her to become me is to give up myself.

I give up myself in speed and strength; my new body has only what nature and evolution saw fit to provide, limbs weak enough to force the brain to better them, with spear and sword and bow, gun and gears and engines, every marvelous creation made by man to compensate for a body barely competent to carry its brain in its head.

I give up myself in mind, abandoning the fluid switch between machine and gray matter that extends myself into others, to disconnect my thoughts to them and theirs to me, to sever the connections that have sustained me. To shut myself off in my own head. To live alone with my thoughts, their echoes muffled in close quarters.

I give myself up in identity as a soldier and an officer and a killer, as a friend and a colleague, and as one by whose hand humanity keeps its place in the universe.

Make no mistake that I am weaker for the loss of each. Make no mistake that I will have to learn again how to fit myself into a world that no longer works like it should. Make no mistake that it will be through force of will alone, that my frustration and anger at being less than what I was will not be visited on you—that even in my newly weakened state I am still dangerous and liable to rage at what I have taken from myself, by becoming this new self.

The woman who opens her eyes in the body I see before me cannot be the same as the one who closes her eyes in the body I have now. Too much changed to remain intact, too much left behind that can't be brought over. I will hold my image of myself to me, but there is only so much of me that will fit.

◆◆◆

If you knew all of this I know you would ask me to consider what I was doing, whether I was sure I was making the right decision, and that you would rather face a life without me than to have me choose a life I would not choose for myself. I know this is what you would say and do as well as I know myself.

And this is why I say with all affection that sometimes you can be such a stupid man. I wouldn't mind you feeling just a little bit greedy for me, that the idea of not having me would make you angry, not heavy-hearted and accepting. There are things you still have to learn about me and this is one of them. It is not that you are too considerate but that I don't mind when you tell me what you want and put that first instead of last.

I don't mind because that is what I am doing now. You should not think I do any of this for you, that I am committing a selfless act or an expression of slavish devotion, that I have signed on for a mermaid's sacrifice and will walk on knives for dumb love. I am too selfish for that. I want you to know that I am here not for you but for me. I want you for my own. I want the life we will have together for my own. I want the silence of peace and release from being the one who walks ten steps ahead of Death. I want the honor of not being feared or hated, and of not having those be the correct response to my presence.

I want to be able to say that I have done my part and I have done it well, but that my part is over and now it is time for my reward, and that reward is you and this life. I want all of this and I am willing to pay to get it.

But it is still hard.

In this I imagine that I am now your equal: You once gave up a life, leaving behind a world and everything on it, all that you had been and everything you knew, on that single sphere of rock and air and water. You put it behind you and stepped into a new life in which you found me. I can't imagine that it was easy to do this.

But was it a sacrifice? Did it take from you more than you could bear? It takes nothing from what you did to say it was not, that you left a life that had

nothing left for you except the marking of tim though it may be, it is not a sacrifice to give for which you no longer have a use.

I am at that place now. This life has m who I am and who I am no longer wants th have seen so much of this universe behind a r a mission. I am ready to see a smaller part depth and in peace. It is not a sacrifice to pay f you want though the price is high. The price new life is everything in the old one. You on up everything in your old life and gained m ready to give up this life and keep you.

◆◆◆

I rest in the container that holds everythi but not anything I will be, and watch as the cian makes her preparations. You are hold hand and telling me of what it was like for y

I smile and I want to kiss you, but not h not now. I do not want a last kiss in an old bc in an old life. I want a first kiss in a new life, a ise fulfilled and no regrets. I am looking forv that kiss. I hold it in my thoughts as I hold there and you there with me.

The technician looks at me now and asks want to begin. I look to you and say I do.

APPENDIX: COMPANY D IN MEMORIAM

In the transcription of ISC/IRI-003-4530/6(C) ("The Sagan Diary"), Lt. Sagan briefly recounts her first mission, the rescue and retrieval of 16th Brigade, Company D, which participated in the Third Battle of Provence. Lt. Sagan's assessment of the tactical qualities of Company D is overly harsh: the official history of the battle (CDFBA/OHR-003-1800/1(A)) clearly indicates that Company D fought tactically and well against a far superior enemy force, and was key in allowing later CDF forces to retake the planet. As acknowledgment of its sacrifice, we note the fallen members of 16th Brigade, Company D here.

Thomas W. Aldrich
Carl Anderson
LaLani Anderson
Will Anderson
Jason Arneaud
Sgt. Sue Arnie
Sean Baeza
Kathryn Baker
Patrick Baker
Nathan P. Bardsley
Kevin Barry
David Baynham
Sean Bell
Spencer Bernard

Moray Binfield
Diane Blum
Eric Bowersox
Joe Brockmeier
Justin Brown
Kevin Brown
Harvey Byas
Jose Cabanillas
Christopher Carrera
Matthew Carroll
Howard Carter
Dave Ciskowski
Joseph Collins
Bruce A. Conklin, Jr.

Karl Cook
Stephen Crowell
Rich Daniels
Christian DeBaun
Griffin T. Demas
Parker B. Demas
Jason Donev
John Doty
Christopher M.
    Downing
Amanda Dwyer
Gerard Fievet
Stephen Fleming
Steven Frame
James Franks
Darren Fry
Juan Fuentes
Janice Galeckas
Matthew Gallagher
Nathan Gendzier
Gerald Getz
Mike Goffee
Samuel Ray Granade
Jeremiah J. Griswold
David Gulick
Christopher Hamilton
Christofer Hardy

Stephen Kennedy
    Harrison
Rodney Haydon
Lorelei Heinmets
Rein Jacob Bandicoot
    Heinmets
Jason Henderson
Tillman James Hodgson
Tatiana Hodziewich
Billy Hollis
Kristian Holvoet
Robert Holz
Jonathan Hoopingarner
David Horst
Eric Howald
Butch Howard
Glenn Howarth
D. Geordie Howe
D. Geordie Howe
    (no relation)
Kenneth Hunt
Robert Jackson
Melissa Jankovic
Randy Johnson
William Johnston
Jason Julier
Mary Kay Kare

Ben Katt

Adam Kearns

Jerry Kelleher

Sean Kelly

David Kirkpatrick

Michael Kranjcevich

Brent Krupp

John C. Kulli

Bobby Kuzma

Ken Nozaki Lacy

Steve Landell

Michael LaSala

Rich Laux

Mathieu Lavigne

Jennifer Leo

Adam Letterman

Allen Lewis

James Lewis

Sean Li

Stephen Lichtwark

Matthew Lindquist

Willem Lohr

Joshua Lopez

John Elliott Lowe IV

Joshua Lowman

John Lowrance

Do-Ming Lum

Susan Mahaffey

Pedro Marroquin

Harry Mayo

Damian McCarthy

Timothy McClanahan

Jason McCulley

Chris McLaren

Phil Merritt

Paul Meyer

Godfrey Milan

Christopher Miller

Jason Mitchell

Stephen Mitchell

P. Janiece Murphy

Michael Myers

Robert Myers

David Nater

Benjamin Nealis

William Nealis

John Needham

Michael Nolan

Patrik Nordebo

Kelly Norton

John O'Neill

Anthony Parisi

John Peitzman

Alex Penchansky

Kurt Perry

Foster Piekarski

Michael A. Porter

Robert Presson

Bryan Price

Michael A. Putlack

Adam Rakunas

David E. Ray

Randall Richmond

John Romkey

Michael Rowley

Karl Sackett

Tomas Sanchez Tejero

Becky Sasala

Jack Savage

James Seals

Ian Seckington

John Clive Edmund Sheffield

Patrick Shepherd

Chris Shipley

Neil A. Shurley

David Smith

Michael Smith

Scot Sonderman

Blaine Spaulding

Hugh Staples

Erik Stegman

Charles Stewart

Stuart Stilborn

Gail Stout

James Courtney Stowe

Jennifer Strachan

Abi Sutherland

Todd Taylor

Charles Terhune

Jason Thurber

Howard Kai-Hao To

Eric Tolladay

Doug Triplett

Lauren Uroff

George Vaughan

Patrick Vera

Lee Walter

Nik Weisend

Bradley G. Wherry

Geraldine Winter

Paul Wood

Paul Worosello

Jody L. Wurl

Todd Yankee

Adam Ziegler

Zane L. Zielinski

AUTHOR
AFTERWORD

On September 25, 2006, science fiction and fantasy author John M. Ford passed away. His loved ones suggested that those who wished to remember him do so by contributing to a book endowment, established in his name, which would benefit the Minneapolis Public Library. I had met Mike Ford only briefly, but a number of good friends and colleagues were close to him, and I wanted to do something to help get the endowment off to a good start. I offered a bound draft version of my novel *The Last Colony* for auction, and noted somewhat jokingly that if the bidding got to $5,000 or above, I would write a short story for the winning bidder, on the grounds that someone who bid that much *deserved* a short story.

As it happens, Bill Schafer of Subterranean Press had been trying to get me to write a story for him, set in my "Old Man's War" universe. So he asked me if I was serious about writing the short story for a $5,000 bid. I said I was; he bid that amount. And here we are: The John M. Ford Book Endowment is $5,000 richer, and I wrote the story you now have in your hands.

I don't want to overstate my relationship with Mike Ford; as I mentioned before, we had met only a few times, although each time was an enjoyable experience. Nevertheless, his warmth and kindness and wit enlightened the lives of people whom I have come to care about in the science fiction community, and their memories and celebration of his life served as an inspiration for me in the writing of this story. I encourage everyone who reads this to seek out his work, which is eminently worth reading.

I'd also like to give a word of appreciation to Bill, whose positive delight in maneuvering me over a barrel to get a story out of me in no way diminishes the generosity of his contribution, which serves both to honor the memory of Mike Ford and puts books in the hands of readers. Bill's a good egg, and I'm delighted he got this story out of me.

—John Scalzi
December 16, 2006